TO MY DAUGHTERS, I love you with all of my heart. The love you share each day warms my heart. Each day is a wonderful journey of love with you. It is a blessing to see you grow in your walk with the Lord.

MY HUSBAND MIKE, thank you for walking with me on my journey in achieving my dream. Each day is a blessing to love and walk with you. I love you.

ENRICO FABRIZI, a great leader, true friend, helper, listener, and advocate. A leader who inspires and encourages. Thanks for your support and belief in a dream from the beginning through each step of the way. Thanks for all you have taught and shared with all those you have led.

PASTOR VIC SCHMELTZ, thank you for helping me grow in my walk with the Lord. Thank you for your guidance in this project.

FINALLY, I'M THANKFUL TO THE LORD for inspiring me to write this book. He opens my heart each day to His great love.

www.mascotbooks.com

15 Days of Love

Second Printing

For more information, please contact:
Mascot Books
620 Herndon Parkway #320
Herndon, VA 20170
info@mascotbooks.com

Library of Congress Control Number: 2017912035

CPSIA Code: PRT0318B
ISBN-13: 978-1-68401-211-4

Printed in the United States

15 DAYS OF LOVE

Kristina Gipe

illustrated by
Ingrid Lefebvre

SOMETIMES others may need a helping hand,

through helping them we can spread love across the land.

We must not rush or put up a fuss,

when others are in need of us.

Many people went to Jesus with great need.

He stopped to help them—taking time not to speed.

LOVE IS PATIENT

We can learn from what He did through following His lead,

by taking time for those around us, we do a great deed.

Jesus showed love for people by His patience for them.

He treated all people as a loving friend.

Who is in need around you today?

Take time for a friend, family member, or neighbor and pray...

God please help me to see those who may be in need around me. Help me to take time for them today, and share the love of Jesus I pray.

LOVE IS KIND

LOVE extends a helping hand to those who are in need.

It's good to serve others by doing a good deed.

To take time for others is kind,

it shows they're on your mind.

Jesus was kind to others by giving of His time,

making Himself available for people to find.

He treated all people with kindness and love,

pleasing His Father in Heaven above.

Kindness helps people see

Jesus' love flowing through you and me.

How can we be kind?

By sharing with and caring for each friend we find.

I HAVE THINGS I want and things I need,
but I know God's best is in store for me.

Friends may have different things than me,
but I must not want strongly that which I see.

God will give me what I need.
I must learn to take Jesus' lead.

LOVE DOES NOT ENVY

Jesus knew God provided for all.
　　We too should trust in God that
　　there is nothing too big or small.

He will help me along the way,
　　I must simply trust in Him and obey.

Take to God your needs in prayer,
　　and trust He will help you get there!

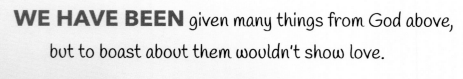

WE HAVE BEEN given many things from God above,
but to boast about them wouldn't show love.

We must be careful not to brag to others about the things we have,
as it may make them feel sad.

When we have things others do not,
we can point them to God and show love by
sharing what we have with them a lot.

IT DOES NOT BOAST

Jesus took time to give thanks and pray,
reminding others of what to say.

Let us give thanks to God above
for all that He has given us and
His great love.

LEARNING TO PUT others before yourself is something we should do,

for it allows the love of Jesus to shine through.

By seeking the needs of others above our own,

we please our Heavenly Father on the throne.

IT IS NOT SELF-SEEKING

Through kindness we show others great love,
    pleasing our Father above.

Jesus gave His life on the cross,
    for the love of humanity, He sought that no lives would be lost.

By committing our lives to God through what Jesus has done,
    we allow Him to work through us to help serve everyone.

It's a beautiful thing to allow God to
use us to help others,
    reaching out to gain in Christ
    sisters and brothers.

LOVE IS REMEMBERING politeness when others speak to me,
for failing to do that would be mean.

Whenever we feel we are being rude,
we should pray to God to help put us in a better mood.

IT IS NOT RUDE

By looking to God, He will help us with what to say,

and can direct us in the right way.

Please and thank you go a long way,

showing love to others and making their day.

JESUS SERVED many people in need,
showing humility by doing a good deed.

He placed the needs of others above His own,
no matter how tired or busy, when others came
He did not moan.

Slowing down for the people around us
is a beautiful thing.
It opens our hearts to a greater
love and the joy that serving
God brings.

To not have pride is to show love,
and we can point many to
God above.

WE SHOULD REMEMBER to not say something that will make someone feel bad,

in the end we will end up feeling sad.

This wouldn't be a good way to show love,

and would not be pleasing to our Heavenly Father above.

When we feel an angry thought come on,

we should talk to God through prayer to help it be gone.

IT IS NOT EASILY ANGERED

We can help solve problems with others by working with them,
and in doing so can create a great friendship in the end.

Jesus did not easily get mad.
His ministry was about love, which made God glad.

SOMETIMES others may say or do things that are mean.
When they do, we must not make a scene.

God forgives us of our sins no matter how big or small,
when we trust in Jesus as our Lord and Savior He gave
His life for us all.

When others do wrong to us we should not fuss,
but take what happened to God and ask Him to help us.

If we hold in our hearts the wrongs others have done,
we miss out on so much in life that is fun.

IT KEEPS NO RECORD OF WRONGS

When we forgive others the wrong they have done,

it shows the world Jesus, teaching them the love of God's son.

His love was great for all,

through Him we learn not to make one another fall.

So, let us forgive others the wrong they have done

and make showing love number one.

LOVE DOES NOT DELIGHT IN EVIL, BUT REJOICES WITH THE TRUTH

WHEN BAD THINGS happen to others, it should not make us glad.

For if we rejoice in others' troubles, it makes our Heavenly Father sad.

The Bible teaches us the truth of God's love.

He cared so much for the whole world He sent His only son from Heaven above.

By dying on the cross, Jesus came to set the world free,

so we can be with Him for eternity.

We should not delight in what is false, but only what is true.

Jesus came to save the world through dying on the cross for me and you.

We should not set our minds on what is bad.

Instead we should think about Jesus and what He did to make our hearts glad.

PROTECTING THOSE around us is a good thing to do.
    From family members to friends, even the animals that bark or moo.

This helps others to see how caring we should be
    and shows the world Jesus through you and me.

The Bible says Jesus was a shepherd protecting the sheep from going astray.
    He saved them from things that could draw them away.

IT ALWAYS PROTECTS

The people were the sheep that Jesus did protect,
the path in which they were to take He did direct.

I can ask God to help protect people when I pray,
and trust that He hears me right away.

WHEN YOU TRUST someone, you believe the words they say are true,
and the plan they have in mind is what they are going to do.

By trusting in Jesus and believing over death He did win,
His love will fill our hearts and wash away our sin.

We can influence others by what we say,
teaching them about Jesus and trusting He is the way.

IT ALWAYS TRUSTS

We can trust in the Lord and His plans for us,

  this will help us to have peace in our heart and
  not to fuss.

Let's make today about the Lord and trust in what
His Word has said,

  and hold forever in our hearts
  all that we have read.

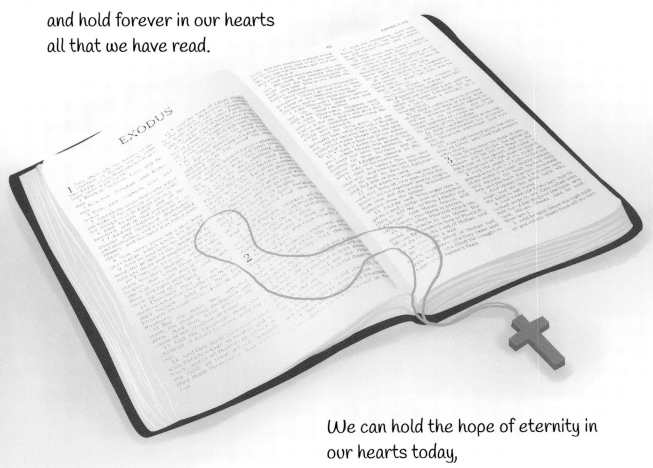

We can hold the hope of eternity in
our hearts today,

  through our love of Jesus and His
  death on the cross being the way.

IT ALWAYS HOPES

HOPE IS when we believe and trust that something will be done.
Love can fill our hearts with hope by trusting in God's son.

By placing our hope in Jesus Christ our lives will not be lost.
He showed great love for all through giving His life on the cross.

Through our love of God we have the hope of eternity,
and that God has made a special place in Heaven for you and me.

Let's make this day a day of hope for all of those we see,
sharing God's message of love and eternity.

ALWAYS PERSEVERES

WHEN WE FACE bad times in life we must always push ahead.

To do so is to hear God's Word and listen to what it says.

To persevere is to keep on trying no matter what's gone wrong,

to pick up your head and hold it high and sing to God in song.

Jesus knew God loved Him and would help Him move ahead.

We can trust the same as well, loving God and what His Word has said.

LOVE NEVER FAILS

LOVE IS when we follow through
   with what we tell people we will do.

When we trust, people will do what they say,
   it shows us they love us and makes our day.

Jesus taught the world about His great love.
   He came down to teach the world from Heaven above.

He taught about love and to watch what you say,
   so you don't fail others and lead them astray.

Jesus gave His life for all to wash away our sin.
   His love will never fail us and we can trust He'll come again.

He told God of what He had need of that day,
   and allowed Him to work in His life always.

When we pray to God to help us each day,
   we can trust He won't fail us and is listening to what we say.

ABOUT THE AUTHOR

KRISTINA GIPE received her Bachelor's Degree in Business, Management, and Economics with a concentration in Business Administration from Empire State College. She felt a tug on her heart from the Lord to write a book and began her writing journey, which later became an undiscovered passion. Writing *15 Days of Love* has been a dream of hers. The Lord inspires Kristina every day to grow in love.